06/06/18

Thank you so Much!
Enjoy the Book!

Chris J

A beautiful day, today would bring.

The sun is beaming and the birds will sing.

We see two kids, the boy's name is Chad.

The girl's name is Jane, and Jane is mad.

Chad was a kid who was always glad.

He just couldn't see why Jane was so mad.

To cheer up his friend, Chad came up with a plan.

"It will work, it has to stand!"

He made silly faces,

sang a silly song,

Even did a handstand that lasted very long.

After two cartwheels, Chad shouted, "Ta dah!'
but Jane shook her head and said, "Stop it, Bah!"

Chad sat down and thought what more he could do.

"Happiness is what she needs, this is true."

Moments later, Chad came back whistling a tune.
In his hand, he showed Jane, was a pink balloon.

Jane stomped the ground and let out an angry shout.

"Stop trying to cheer me up!
PLEASE CUT IT OUT!"

Chad was crushed that he couldn't cheer up his friend.
Suddenly, a man appeared and shook Chad's hand.

The man smiled warmly and said,
"You're a great friend to Jane, Chad"
Jane saw the man and said, "Dad?"

Jane ran to her dad and hugged him real tight.

"I missed you, Dad," she said.

"I missed you too, Jane.

Everything is now alright."

Jane was now smiling, no longer mad, sad, or blue.
Jane's dad looked at both kids and asked,
"What would you two like to do?"

They made silly faces,

sang a silly song,

Jane, her dad, and Chad
played all day long.

Time flew by and now it was getting dark.

Jane looked at Chad and said,
"Sorry for being mean, my friend. You are all heart."

Chad gave his friend a big hug and was taken home by Jane's dad. From his window, he was happy to see that Jane was no longer mad.

Made in the USA
Lexington, KY
18 May 2018